SPAGHETTI FOR SUZY
PETA COPLANS

Andersen Press · London

For Cleo and Adam

This paperback edition first published in 2003 by Andersen Press Ltd.
Copyright © 1992 by Peta Coplans. The rights of Peta Coplans to be identified as the author and illustrator of this work have been asserted by her in accordance with the Copyright, Designs and Patents Act, 1988. First published in Great Britain in 1992 by Andersen Press Ltd. 20 Vauxhall Bridge Road, London SW1V 2SA. Published in Australia by Random House Australia Pty., 20 Alfred Street, Milsons Point, Sydney, NSW 2061. Colour separated in Switzerland by Photolitho, Zürich. All rights reserved. Printed and bound in Italy by Grafiche AZ, Verona.

10 9 8 7 6 5 4 3 2 1

British Library Cataloguing in Publication Data available.

ISBN 1 84270 100 2

This book has been printed on acid-free paper

Suzy liked lots of things – dogs, cats, balloons, fun-fairs and crazy bows in her hair.

At the park Suzy liked to build the highest castle in the sand-pit . . .

. . . and then squash it flat.

Most of all, Suzy liked spaghetti. She ate it every day.
"One day she'll get tired of it," her mum said.

But she didn't. Soon she wouldn't eat anything else.

Every morning Suzy's mum cooked her a mountain of spaghetti.

By bedtime it was gone.
"She'll turn into a noodle soon," her dad said. But she didn't.

In the park one day, Suzy met a cat.
"Spaghetti! Just what I need!" said the cat.

He took a long piece . . .

What do you think he did with it?

Later, Suzy met a pig.
"Spaghetti! Just what I need!" said the pig, taking two
pieces . . .

What do you think he did with them?

Along came a dog.
"Spaghetti! Just what I need!" said the dog.

He emptied the whole bowlful into his bag . . .

What do you think he did with it?

"Thanks for the spaghetti," said Suzy's friends when they came back.

"We thought you might be hungry."

Suzy looked at the fruit. The animals looked at Suzy.

"Why fruit?" asked Suzy. "I only like spaghetti."

"Apples taste of windy autumn days," said the pig.

"Cherries taste of country picnics," said the cat.

"And bananas," said the dog, "bananas taste of the wild, green jungle."

"Hmm!" said Suzy, and she ate the fruit. "ALMOST as good as spaghetti!"

"I'm still hungry," said Suzy. "We're ALL hungry!"
said the dog.

"Well, come on," said Suzy. "What are we waiting for?"

"Spaghetti for everyone!" said Suzy.

And what do you think they did with it?

More Andersen Press paperback picture books!